TILLY'S PONY TAILS

Lucky Chance
the new foal

D1453333

TILLY'S PONY TAILS

Lucky Chance
the new foal

PIPPA FUNNELL

Illustrated by Jennifer Miles

Orion
Children's Books

First published in Great Britain in 2009
by Orion Children's Books
a division of the Orion Publishing Group Ltd
Orion House
5 Upper St Martin's Lane
London WC2H 9EA
An Hachette UK Company

5 7 9 8 6 4

A catalogue record for this book is available from the British Library.

ISBN 978 1 84255 713 6

www.orionbooks.co.uk
www.tillysponytails.co.uk

For my goddaughter,
Isabelle Cook

One

It was nearly the end of the Easter holidays
which, for Tilly Redbrow and her friends at
Silver Shoe Farm, meant one thing: the
countdown to Pony Club camp
had started. Tilly was keen to
get as much riding practice as
possible before her first camp,
so she'd asked Angela, her
instructor, and the owner of
Silver Shoe Farm, to give
her extra lessons.

7

That evening they were working on her canter. Angela was reminding Tilly how to use her legs and voice to instruct Rosie, the strawberry roan pony she shared with Mia.

"You're looking more confident, Tilly," Angela called. "Keep encouraging her forward with the leg, and avoid the temptation to pull on the reins. Soften both arms a bit more."

Tilly relaxed her arms, and squeezed gently with her lower leg.

"Come on, Rosie," she said. "Come on, girl."

Rosie followed Tilly's instruction without hesitation, and they completed two circuits of the sand school, as Angela watched.

"That's it! Grow a little taller. Keep those shoulders back and try not to drive with your seat!"

Tilly immediately straightened up, but when she caught sight of Mia waving frantically from the fence, she lost concentration.

"Hey, guys! Come quick. Duncan thinks Lulabelle is going to give birth soon!"

This was exciting news because the vet had said it was unlikely she would be able to have a foal. Lulabelle was a Welsh-bred mare who had been sent to Silver Shoe Farm two years ago by the charitable organisation, World Horse Welfare. She was the worst of five horses Angela had found in a terrible condition on a remote farm. Lulabelle wasn't the first horse Angela had re-homed, and she certainly wouldn't be the last.

"I'd better go and see what's happening," said Angela. "Why don't you and Mia take Rosie back to the stables and then come and

join us. Hopefully the vet's already on his way."

Tilly jumped down from Rosie and led her through the gate.

"I can't believe it's happening," said Mia, walking beside them, breathless with excitement. "A new foal, here at Silver Shoe Farm!"

"What's happened so far?" asked Tilly keenly.

"Duncan's been checking on her every half hour for the last twenty-four hours – he looks really tired. He said he thought she was about to foal because she was producing lots of milk and she didn't want to be near any of the other horses. They're in the back barn, where it's nice and quiet."

Tilly glanced at her watch.

"But it's nearly seven. My dad's coming to pick me up in ten minutes."

"Phone him and tell him he can't!" said Mia. "He'll have to come later."

Quickly Tilly called her dad. She pleaded with him to let her stay and watch the birth. He was worried about homework and late nights making Tilly too tired for starting back at school.

"But this is *like* being at school, Dad," she explained. "It's educational!"

In the end, he agreed.

"Phew!" said Tilly.

The girls knew they had to be quiet when they approached the barn. Duncan and Angela were watching from the door.

"Where's the foal then?" whispered Mia impatiently.

"She hasn't broken her waters yet," said Duncan. "But it's going to happen soon. Foaling usually happens any time between 10pm and 4am, so it could be a long night. If you girls want to help, a flask of tea would be great . . ."

Tilly and Mia trooped over to the club room. They made enough tea for everyone and poured it into a thermos flask.

"Do you think the foal will be male or female?" asked Mia, opening a packet of biscuits.

"Hmm . . . I think it's going to be a filly," said Tilly. "I don't know why, I've just got a hunch."

"We'll see. There's so much happening – a foal for Easter, and then camp next holidays. Are you looking forward to it?"

"I can't wait."

"It's going to be the best ever. We'll get

to spend the week with Cally – she's taking
Mr Fudge. We'll have such a good laugh."

Just thinking about it made Tilly's
stomach flutter with excitement. She was
looking forward to seeing Cally too. Cally
used to ride at Silver Shoe Farm until she
moved to Cavendish Hall, the exclusive
boarding school near North Cosford. The
camp was going to bring them back
together again.

"Let's go and see how Lulabelle is
getting on," said Mia.

The girls carried the flask and biscuits to
the barn. As they got near, Duncan
beckoned them over and whispered,

"Her placenta has ruptured!"

"Oh no!" said Mia, alarmed.

"No, no. It's a good thing," he said. "It's
supposed to happen. It means labour has
started. Come and look."

Tilly shivered with anticipation. She crept up to the door of the barn and peered over. Lulabelle was lying on her side, on a bed of straw. The air inside seemed perfectly still and quiet, as though something magical was about to happen. Lulabelle didn't seem to mind that people were watching. In fact, she hardly seemed aware of them at all. She looked peaceful. Tilly imagined she was thinking about meeting her baby. Nothing else mattered.

"Do we need to do anything?" she asked.

"We aren't going to interfere if we can help it," said Angela. "Hopefully nature will do its thing, and Belle can deliver her foal all by herself. The vet's not far away if we need him."

Twenty minutes later, Lulabelle began to push. She groaned a little, and as she did, a smooth, thin white sac appeared. Within the sac was the first glimpse of the foal. Its front hooves came out first, one slightly ahead of the other, and then

gradually the nose and head were pushed out.

Tilly stared, open-mouthed. She'd never seen anything like it before.

After a little rest, Lulabelle continued pushing. Next came the shoulders and body, followed by the hips and back legs. At last, the foal was out in the world. It rested with its mother for fifteen minutes or so, and during that time, no one said a word. Everyone was happy just to watch.

Eventually, Lulabelle stood up, breaking the umbilical cord, and although it caused some bleeding, Duncan assured the girls that this was fine. It took a number of very wobbly attempts before the newborn finally stood up, but Tilly couldn't quite believe how quickly the foal was able to get to its feet.

At this point, Duncan stepped in and dipped the foal's belly in iodine solution to prevent infection, and then turned it towards its mother to encourage it to feed.

"I think we've got ourselves a filly!" he said proudly.

Tilly studied the helpless little creature – she had weak bandy legs and a scrawny body. She could barely keep herself upright. It seemed strange to think that one day she'd be big and strong, like Magic Spirit. But of course she would be.

"What shall we call her?" asked Angela.

Tilly thought about this for a moment. She knew that Lulabelle had been lucky to

spend time at Silver Shoe, overcoming her neglect and poor condition. And it had only been by chance that Angela happened to have a smart stallion in for schooling at the same time Lulabelle was in season.

"Lucky Chance," she said confidently.

"Perfect!" said Angela, and everyone agreed.

Two

Lucky Chance was in Tilly's thoughts
constantly, which made the build up to
Pony Club camp go pleasantly fast. Every
evening after school she went to the farm
and checked on her progress.

In a very short time Lucky changed
so much. Her coat dried out and her fuzzy
mane began to stick up. She stayed close
to Lulabelle, and looked tiny next to her –
even though she was growing daily. Tilly
loved the way her body and head seemed

too big for her spindly legs, and that her enormous knees stuck out like tennis balls.

As the weeks went by, the weather improved and the evenings became lighter. Life at Silver Shoe Farm continued to be as busy as ever. The stable yard was always buzzing with the usual mucking out, feeding and grooming routines, and as the girls went about their work, there was constant chatter about camp.

June was ideal for sunny evening hacks. Tilly made sure she did plenty of those, joining Mia for explorations of the tracks and bridlepaths around the farm. But whenever she could, she went down to the long field to see Lucky Chance. The good weather meant Lucky could spend more time at pasture. The exercise helped with her development and it was funny watching her try to keep up with Lulabelle.

Tilly didn't want Rosie or Magic Spirit to feel left out, so she made sure she spent time with them too. The days flew by and in no time at all it was time for camp. On Friday evening – the day before camp – she groomed Magic Spirit before going to watch his training session with Duncan.

As she brushed, she told him all about Lucky Chance's progress.

"It's amazing, Magic. That tiny little newborn has become a confident young foal. She's walking around the field and mixing with the other mares. Hey, maybe she'll be a champion one day – what do you think?"

Magic lifted his head and pricked his ears forward.

"Was that a yes or a no? Oh, never mind! You'll have to look after Lucky Chance while I'm away at camp. She's the newest kid on the block, so you'll need to make sure she's happy and safe. You'd make a good step-dad. And she's so tiny and you're so big. I'm trusting *you*, Magic."

With that, Magic turned and gave Tilly a friendly nudge with his nose. Tilly took this as a positive response. She loved chatting to him about all sorts of things. If she had a problem or worry, he was the first to know. If she had some news or a funny story she always shared it with him during grooming sessions. In some ways, he was her best friend.

"Okay," she said, patting his neck. "Time to meet Duncan. He says you're going to practise transitions today."

Tilly attached a lead rope to Magic's head collar, led him across the yard, and tied him up in the wash box ready for tacking up. She thought about how far Magic had come since his arrival at Silver Shoe Farm as a rescue horse. He'd been in a terrible condition then – underfed and covered in sores, and it had taken lots of care and patience to build up his health. Then, just a few months ago, he'd had a bout of colic, which had been a very scary time. The vet couldn't be certain that Magic would pull through, but with Tilly's special attention, he'd made a full recovery. And now he'd been lunged and backed, it was only a matter of time before he'd be ready for Tilly to try. It was an exciting thought. With his toned physique and glossy coat, he looked like a winner, the kind of horse that would make it to the top.

Riding Magic was something Tilly couldn't wait to do. That really would feel like a dream coming true. She knew she had to be patient though. Duncan and Angela wouldn't let her do it until they were certain Magic would carry her safely.

Duncan came in carrying a saddle and a snaffle bridle.

"Let's get this on him," he said.

Tilly helped place the saddle on Magic's back and secure it in place, while Duncan put on the bridle.

Once tacked up, Duncan got on and took Magic towards the outdoor school. As they walked, Duncan kept changing Magic's direction, making small circles and loops. He wanted to concentrate on Magic's

basic steering and, every so often, would ask him to halt using his voice, as well as other aids.

"I want him to step forward and up into the halt transition," he explained to Tilly. "If I use my hands too much as I close my leg, he'll resist me, so I've got to be quick to soften the rein as soon as I've asked for the transition, then tighten my seat slightly so his back can come up. If I sit too heavy, he'll just hollow his back and resist."

Magic soon worked out what Duncan was asking for. It wasn't the neatest halt in the world, but Tilly was impressed. She was also impressed by how quiet and patient Duncan was.

"It looked as if you hardly did anything," she remarked.

"Steady in the seat, soft with the hands – that's the best approach," said Duncan. "Sometimes you might see riders halt their horses by hauling back on the reins and ripping on their mouths in the process. But if a horse is trained properly, he'll learn to respond to very soft, light aids, and hearing the word 'whoa'. There's no need to yank the reins. Watch . . ."

Duncan performed the exercise again, and this time Magic was quicker to respond. They did it several times over, and eventually Magic was stopping neatly and squarely, as if he was a horse with years of experience.

"Good boy!" called Tilly proudly. She loved watching these training sessions, because they taught her so much about horsemanship. She was hungry to learn and Silver Shoe Farm was the ideal place to do it.

Just as Tilly was getting ready to leave, Angela came over.

"Before you go," she said. "Would you mind moving Lucky and Belle to the small field for me?"

"No problem," said Tilly. She was happy to do it.

She found Lucky and Belle grazing together in the shade. She haltered Belle

and as soon as she starting leading her towards the gate, Lucky followed.

"It won't be long before you're wearing your own halter," she told Lucky, as they walked through to the next field. "You're growing so fast. I'm going to miss you so much while I'm at camp."

Three

The day before camp, Tilly sat in her room and organised her packing. She spread everything across the carpet, and texted Cally and Mia to check that she had what she needed:

HI. HOW MANY PAIRS OF JODHPURS DO U THINK I
NEED? T. XXX

Cally replied straightaway:

AS MANY AS U'VE GOT! X

Tilly looked at her collection.
Together she had three pairs. The ones
Cally had given her when she first joined
Silver Shoe Farm; the cool denim-look pair
her mum and dad had given her for her
birthday; and a new fake suede seated
beige pair that her Auntie Jackie had
bought her especially for her first Pony
Club camp.

Suddenly, Tilly's mum appeared at the
door.

"I just wanted to check you've got
everything you need," she said, smiling.
She came in and sat down on Tilly's bed.

"Look at all this stuff! I hope your bag
is big enough. Are you excited?"

Tilly nodded.

"It's the first time you've been away on
your own, Tilly. So grown up. I'm sure
you'll love every minute!"

Tilly joined her mum on the bed and gave her a hug. Suddenly she felt a bit like Lucky, wanting to follow Belle everywhere. She'd been so busy thinking about what to take and what she was going to do when she got there, that she had forgotten she was going to be away from her mum and dad for a whole week.

"It's a big adventure," said her mum, stroking her hair. "It's fine to feel a bit nervous. But Cally and Mia will look after you. And you can always phone us, okay?"

"Thanks, Mum."

Tilly smiled. She pictured herself and Rosie parading around the yard – there would be all sorts of games and activities. She knew everyone would be sleeping in dormitories, and Mia had told her that there would be midnight feasts every night.

"Before you go," said her mum slowly, "I want to give you something."

She reached into her pocket and pulled out a crumpled photo, then handed it to Tilly. It was a picture of a young woman with long dark hair, standing next to a stunning black horse. The woman was wearing cowboy boots and a fringed top. She looked like a Native American.

"Who's that?" said Tilly.

"Well . . . that's your real mum."

Tilly gasped.

"The social worker at the children's home gave us this photo, along with your special horsehair bracelet, when we adopted you. You're old enough to have this now and I think you should."

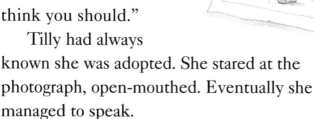

Tilly had always known she was adopted. She stared at the photograph, open-mouthed. Eventually she managed to speak.

"Sh-she looks just like me."

"Yes, she does. You've got her eyes and her hair," said her mum. "And look at the horse. Everyone's been saying what a natural you are around the horses at Silver Shoe Farm, and now you're going off to your very first Pony Club camp, I just thought you should see this. It looks like you and your real mum both had a special gift with horses."

"It's wonderful," said Tilly. "It all makes sense, doesn't it? The reason I love

horses so much is because my real mum did."

"I think you're right," said her mum, and kissed the top of her head. "I'm so proud of you, Tilly."

"And I'm proud to be a Redbrow. You're the best mum in the world!"

That night, Tilly lay awake in bed. Her packing was all done, and her suitcase looked as though it was about to burst. So much was happening: the arrival of Lucky Chance, Pony Club camp, the photograph of her real mum – no wonder she couldn't sleep. Moonlight streamed in through the curtains. Thankfully, it

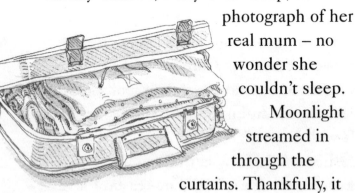

was a cool night. Magic Spirit and Rosie would be comfortable in their stables. Lucky Chance would be sleeping beside her mum. Tilly's phone beeped. It was a message from Mia.

R U AWAKE? CAN'T SLEEP. TOO EXCITED. X

Tilly sat up and replied:

ME TOO. GOT LOTS TO TELL U! I WONDER HOW ROSIE
IS FEELING? X

Seconds later, Mia replied:

BET SHE'S EXCITED TOO! X

Tilly put her phone down and climbed out of bed. She went over to her suitcase and opened it. On top was the crumpled photograph. She picked it up and stared at it. Immediately, her mind was flooded with questions. What was her real mum's name? How old was she in this picture? Why was she wearing cowboy boots and that fringed top? Where did the horse come from? It was a very handsome animal, strong and bold. It almost looked like a wild horse. And what was that around her wrist? It looked like a bracelet, but it was hard to tell. Maybe it was the one she'd been found with?

Tilly played with her horsehair bracelet and wondered whether the hairs in it came from the horse in the photograph. She wore it next to the bracelet made from Magic Spirit's tail hair, the one that her adoptive mum had made her – it felt as though history was catching up with the present.

She couldn't wait to tell Cally and Mia all about it. There was only one way to make the waiting go faster, of course. She climbed back into bed, lay down, closed her eyes, and thinking about Magic and Lucky Chance, she *tried* her hardest to fall asleep.

Four

"Here it comes!" said Mia, as the Pony Club bus swerved into the driveway. Everyone crowded towards it, keen to get on and get going. Tilly and Mia stayed close to Cally, who had promised she was going to be an honorary Silver Shoe girl for the week – being together again felt great.

Tilly kissed her mum and dad goodbye, and gave Adam a hug. Scruff looked up at her and wagged his tail, so she gave him a hug too. The girls put their cases in the luggage compartment and climbed on board. They managed to get seats at the back, which Mia insisted were definitely the best on the bus.

"How many others are on here, do you reckon?" asked Tilly, staring at the rows of heads.

"I heard someone say that there are forty of us," answered Cally.

"They're all members of the Cosford Pony Club branch. I know lots of them from Cavendish Hall," added Cally.

"Cool!" said Tilly. "I bet they've got amazing horses!"

"It's no big deal," shrugged Cally. "Come on, I'll introduce you to some of them."

Cally called out to a group of girls sitting a few rows ahead of them.

"Eleanor! Jessica! Hiya!"

Two fair-haired girls turned around, kneeled up on their seats and grinned.

"Hi, Cally! How are you? How's Mr Fudge?"

"He's great," said Cally. "He's coming to camp. Are you still riding Curby?"

"Yep. Did you hear? She won the regional finals on Saturday. And Jessica's pony, Nightshade, came second."

Jessica, the taller of the two girls, smiled proudly.

"Well done," said Cally.

"Thanks! Are you guys sharing a room?"

"Yeah. Maybe we can get a big one together. These are my friends, Mia and Tilly," said Cally. "Tilly's only just joined the Pony Club, so this is her first camp."

Tilly waved and gave a little smile.

"Hi, Tilly. I love your hair. It's so long!"

"All the way down my back!" Tilly said.

"Wow! I wish I could grow my hair that long," said Eleanor.

Tilly was relieved that Eleanor and Jessica seemed so friendly. She looked forward to seeing their prize-winning ponies.

Eventually the bus pulled away. Tilly, Mia and Cally waved at their mums and dads, but generally they were too excited to be sad about saying goodbye. The organisers, Bob and Margaret, made an announcement over the loudspeaker system, welcoming everyone, and the whole bus cheered – although everyone groaned when Bob told them that mobile phones weren't allowed.

"Bob and Margaret are really nice," whispered Cally. "But watch out, because Bob's really fussy about clean tack and grooming. Last year, he moaned at Mia constantly. Each team can earn points for good turn-out."

The journey took over an hour. Along the way they sang pop songs and gossiped about who was going to be sharing rooms.

"How many boys are there?" asked Tilly.

"I counted four," said Cally. "The twins are here – remember them from last year? And then there's a new boy in the front row; he looks a bit scared."

"Wouldn't you be, surrounded by hundreds of pony-crazed girls?!" laughed Mia. "Hey – do you think *you-know-who* is here?" she winked.

"You mean," nodded Cally, ". . . *him*?"

"*Who*?" said Tilly.

"Brook Ashton-Smith!" said Mia, rolling her eyes. "Do you remember we met him when we visited Cavendish Hall with Cally? He played the drums and had that amazing horse . . ."

"You mean Solo?" said Tilly. "The black thoroughbred?"

She remembered the meeting clearly. She had used her whispering skills to help Brook sort out a problem with Solo's jumping. She was looking forward to talking to him again, and finding out how Solo was getting on.

"Brook is so hot!" added Mia.

"Shame he's older than us," said Cally. "I think he must be about sixteen, so he'll be in the senior group. He's been to camp every year. Look, there he is . . ."

Cally pointed towards a group of chattering heads at the front of the bus. There were six or seven of them. Tilly spotted Brook immediately. He had short dark hair and olive skin, and when he smiled his whole face lit up.

"We'll have to talk to him later," said Mia.

At last the bus arrived at Barton House, which was an enormous training centre near a river. The main building was made of grey stone and looked like a creepy castle.

"The dormitories are supposed to be haunted!" said Jessica.

Fortunately, the rest of the surroundings were more cheerful. There was even a swimming pool, which could be used in the evenings.

Once everyone had unloaded from the bus, they had to find their way to the feed

room, tack room and stables. Each item of gear had its own storage space, but it was hard work organising the heavy things such as sacks of feed, saddles and suitcases.

The horses weren't arriving till later, so there was time for everyone to find their bedrooms in the main house. Tilly and her friends crept along a dark corridor until they came to a door, which had their names on it.

"Excellent!" said Mia. "The three of us are together, sharing with Eleanor and Jessica . . . and someone called Sabrina."

Eleanor and Jessica were close behind, lugging their heavy bags.

They all piled into the room. It was basic and cold, with three sets of bunk beds and a cracked sink.

"Ew! It smells funny!" moaned Eleanor.

"It's not exactly luxury!" said Mia.

"Oh well, you know what Margaret always says," Cally said, smiling.

"Your pony's comfort is more important than your own!" the girls chanted together.

"As long as we have a good time," shrugged Tilly, "I don't mind where we sleep."

"I wonder where Sabrina is," said Mia. "Does anyone know her?

"Yeah, she's in our year at Cavendish Hall," said Jessica "She's all right, but she's a bit . . . fussy. She won't like this room, that's for sure."

Just as Jessica finished her sentence, the door flung open. A tall girl with lip-gloss and hair extensions stood in the entrance, snarling.

"*This* is unbelievable! If they think I'm going to spend a single night in this *dump*, they can think again! It's not on! I'm phoning my dad!"

She pulled out her mobile and started pounding the buttons.

"Naughty, naughty – remember what Bob said," giggled Mia. "No mobiles!"

Meanwhile, Jessica and the others gave each other I-told-you-so smiles, and started to unpack their things.

Five

The horses arrived just after three o'clock, but before they were unloaded, the girls had to prepare the stables by laying down bedding and making sure that there was water and hay.

"I can't wait to see Mr Fudge," said Cally, as she tied up a hay-net. "He gets so excited when he visits a new place. And Rosie, I've missed her so much. Look – I'm still wearing the bracelet you made me."

47

Cally held up her wrist to show Tilly.

"Hey!" said Mia, joining them. "Nice bracelet, Cally. You two match – Silver Shoe Farm for ever!"

"Always!" agreed Cally.

"I can't wait to see Rosie either," said Tilly, thinking she'd make Mia a special bracelet too, as soon as she got the chance. "I've got some of her favourite treats with me."

She reached into her pocket for a handful of mints.

48

"She'll deserve them after such a long
journey."

When they were ready, everyone
gathered in the yard, where the horseboxes
were parked. The atmosphere buzzed, as
they all eagerly anticipated seeing their
horses and ponies again. Tilly watched and
admired each one as they were led from
the trailers and collected by their owners.

There were some beautiful animals, all
different colours and markings. Some of
them were very athletic looking, more like
eventers or show jumpers. They made
Rosie look a bit scruffy.

"What a striking horse!" said a voice
behind Tilly. "That horse has got so much
presence – he really stands out!"

It was Bob. He was admiring a large
black thoroughbred with powerful back
legs and a neat mane. Tilly recognised the
horse instantly.

"That's Solo," she whispered to Cally.
"Apparently his father was a top race horse.
Isn't he gorgeous?"

49

"Not as gorgeous as his owner," sniggered Mia, overhearing.

Eventually, Tilly and Mia's names were called and Rosie was unloaded from her trailer. She looked tired but happy to be outside again. They greeted her and gave her a peppermint before leading her across the yard to the stables. They had agreed

that Tilly would do most of the riding on Rosie, and Mia, being more experienced, would be borrowing a ride from the camp organisers.

"Welcome to your holiday home," Tilly said, as she removed Rosie's travelling boots and rug, and made sure she was comfortable. Along the corridor of stables,

she could hear other riders saying similar things to their horses.

Once the horses were settled, the campers had to go to a meeting in the lecture room, where they were going to be told about the week's activities and introduced to the camp instructors.

"You'll get the chance to learn and improve your skills in dressage, cross-country, show jumping, mounted games, hacks, and lots more," explained Margaret.

"Don't expect it to be easy," warned Bob. "As most of you know, Pony Club camp is lots of fun, but it's also hard work. You'll be responsible for your horses throughout the week – this means you do all the mucking out, feeding, and grooming. And after your riding lessons, you'll have a tack cleaning session with me. No slacking!

We'll be dividing you into riding groups now, so listen out for your name."

Everyone waited patiently to find out which riding group they were in. Brook and the older people were all in the senior group together. Tilly was pleased to hear that her group would be the people she was sharing a room with. The six of them gathered round and were introduced to their instructor.

"Hi, I'm Naomi," said the young woman. "This is my third year as an instructor at Barton House. So if there's anything you need to know, just ask. Alarms are set for 7am, so that you can muck out and feed your ponies before breakfast."

"Oooh, I'd forgotten about that," Mia groaned.

"Where can I get a softer pillow?" asked Sabrina. "The one they've given me is really lumpy."

"Um, I'm sure you'll get used to it," said Naomi flatly.

Sabrina sat back and sulked.

"How often do we get to ride?" asked Tilly.

"Twice a day. There's a session in the morning and one in the afternoon. Some of it will be formal instruction, and some of it will be fun and games – there's a lot to be said for just getting out and having fun with your horse."

Tilly grinned. She couldn't believe she would be riding twice a day for a whole week.

When the meeting came to an end it was time for dinner. As the girls walked across the yard, towards the main house,

the senior campers walked beside them.

"Hi, Brook," said Cally and Mia.

Brook looked at them, and then he smiled.

"Oh, hi, girls! How are you? Good to see

you've come to camp. Hiya, Tilly, I thought it was you."

He gave Tilly an extra friendly grin, and Cally and Mia nudged her.

Dinner was served in the dining hall: lasagne and garlic bread, followed by jam roly-poly and custard. Tilly thought it was tasty, but by the time she was sitting at the dining table, she was almost too tired to eat.

After dinner, the girls went to their bedroom. Tilly agreed to share a bunk with Sabrina, and said she didn't mind sleeping on top.

"Thanks, Tilly," said Sabrina. "I really don't like heights. They make me feel queasy."

"How do you cope with being up on a horse then?" snapped Mia.

"That's *different*."

Eventually the girls got into their sleeping bags but before they went to sleep, they shared a bag of sweets and Tilly showed them the photograph of her mum.

She explained how she'd been adopted and didn't know anything about her background except that her mum must have been interested in horses.

"That's amazing," said Cally. "Do you think that's where your talent with horses comes from?"

"Maybe," said Tilly, staring at the ceiling. "I guess I'll never know for sure." As she closed her eyes, she felt so good, knowing that her mum and dad loved her, and that her birth mum shared her passion for horses.

Six

At 7am the alarm clocks buzzed. The girls crawled out of their sleeping bags, and stumbled about the room, pulling on their boots and jackets over their pyjamas.

"I feel like I've not even been to bed," croaked Tilly.

"It's outrageous! I'm not having it!" said Mia, mimicking Sabrina.

By half past seven they were down at the stables, feeding their ponies and mucking out. Hardly anyone spoke, except to say hello to their horses.

"You're like a bunch of zombies!" said Naomi, the instructor, who was supervising the activity. "Come on – a decent breakfast should wake you all up!"

They trooped back to the dining hall and sat in long rows. Once the orange juice had been passed around, the conversation began – eager chatter about what would be happening during the morning.

"Usually we try something different each lesson," said Jessica. "I like cross-country the best."

"I like the mounted games," said Mia. "But I *hate* dressage. That's my worst thing."

Tilly was thrilled at the thought of practising all these different activities, but like Mia, she was also worried about the dressage. It always looked so complicated.

"I *love* dressage," said Sabrina proudly. "I'm really good at it."

The others just rolled their eyes.

Slices of buttery toast disappeared from the table as fast as they arrived. Everyone was hungry after the early start. Some people had sausages, eggs and bacon. Tilly went for her usual: muesli and milk with a chopped banana.

After breakfast it was straight up to the rooms to change for riding, then back to the stables to groom the horses and get tacked up.

"Take good care," warned Cally. She was in the stable next door to Tilly, grooming Mr Fudge. "Do everything as neatly as possible, because before lessons start, there's an inspection of tack and turn-out. Let's get points for our group."

Tilly made sure she was extra careful, but Rosie's thick mane and tail never looked very smart.

"Oh well, you're still lovely," she sighed.

Lessons began at ten o'clock. The girls led their ponies towards the arena, and waited for Naomi to ask them to mount. Tilly hadn't felt nervous until now, but as she glanced at Jessica, Eleanor and Sabrina, standing confidently next to their horses, she felt butterflies in her stomach. She knew she was the least experienced of the group, and hoped she wouldn't make lots of mistakes.

Once they had mounted, Naomi watched the six girls trot their ponies round the arena. She gave them tips and suggestions to help improve their balance and posture, as they went by.

"Keep your legs down beneath you, Cally. Remember that imaginary line drawn between your shoulders, hip and heel. Head up, eyes looking ahead. Good."

But Eleanor's pony, Curby, wouldn't behave himself. He found it very exciting being in a group lesson.

"It looks like he's doing the Riverdance!" laughed Mia.

"He's just showing off," said Eleanor. "Maybe he thinks this is boring!"

As Tilly trotted round with Rosie she tried to remember everything that Angela had taught her. She kept her arms relaxed and her shoulders back. She focused on her balance and visualised a continuous line from her elbow all the way to the bit in Rosie's mouth. Rosie was very responsive.

"Looking great up there, Tilly," said Naomi. "I hear you haven't been riding for very long."

"No, this is my first Pony Club camp."

"Well, you've obviously been working hard and listening to your instructor. You look very established for someone who's just starting out."

Tilly grinned from ear to ear. Angela would be so proud. She couldn't wait to tell her.

Thinking about Angela, Tilly started to wonder what was happening back at Silver

Shoe. She pictured Lucky Chance following Belle around the pasture, enjoying the sunshine. Maybe Lucky was practising her trot. Had Angela decided to train her to lead yet? Tilly didn't like the idea of missing anything, so when no one was looking she hid behind a fence post and sent a quick text to Duncan:

HEY! WHAT'S HAPPENING?
HAVE U BEEN RIDING MAGIC?
HOW IS LUCKY? T. X

Duncan replied straightaway, which was a relief because Tilly didn't want to get caught breaking the no-mobiles rule, even if it was for an extremely important Silver Shoe update.

ALL WELL. MAGIC MISSING YOU.
LUCKY HAS BEEN SNIFFING MANURE!
SHE'S CURIOUS ABOUT EVERYTHING –
QUITE A CHARACTER. ENJOY CAMP.
DUNCAN.

It was good to hear that nothing major had happened without her, although the manure sniffing sounded quite funny. And as for Magic missing her, well, she knew that anyway, because she was missing him too.

Seven

At midday the girls ate a lunch of hot-dogs and salad, and then helped to wash the dishes. Soon it was time for their second ride of the day.

"Good news, guys," Naomi announced. "This afternoon we're going to do some cross-country practice. Make sure you all put your crash helmets and body protectors on."

"Hooray!" the girls cheered.

"Maybe Curby will behave himself now," said Eleanor. "Cross-country is his thing."

They led their ponies towards the cross-country course, which was set in the beautiful parkland of Barton House.

"No one has to do anything they're not comfortable with," Naomi explained. "But let's give each other lots of encouragement. Cross-country success is mostly to do with confidence. Before we start, I want everyone to put their stirrup leathers up two holes from normal show jumping length."

"Ugh, I *hate* riding with short stirrups," Sabrina groaned.

"This will make it easier for you to stay balanced," Naomi explained, ignoring Sabrina. "Between fences I want you to stand up in your stirrups, as you'll have seen jockeys do, but then you're going to bring your seat back to the saddle four or five strides before each fence.

"With cross-country, it's essential you don't get in front of your horse or pony. By that I mean too far forward with your balance, because if your pony stops, hits a fence, or stumbles on landing, it's more than likely you'll end up on the ground."

There were all sorts of cross-country fences set out – the Pony Club had made full use of the park's lovely natural features. Steps had been transformed into mounds; there were logs, brush fences, little corner fences, arrowheads, and ditches. Tilly thought it looked just like a miniature version of Badminton!

"We're just going to work on three or four fences at a time today," said Naomi. "We'll all watch one another and learn from our mistakes."

Mia was the first to have a go, riding Sweetie, the pony she was borrowing from the camp, and she jumped neatly over a couple of logs and a brush fence, then over a small step on to a bank.

"I love it!" she cried, as she returned to the others. The girls cheered her in – especially Tilly. She'd never seen Mia jump so well.

"Would you like to try it now?" asked Naomi, smiling at Tilly.

"Um . . . yeah . . . um . . ."

Tilly hesitated. She wanted to, but she was worried. She'd never jumped a solid fence before; she'd only jumped fences that knocked down.

"Go for it, Tilly!" said Jessica. "Just take it step by step."

"Okay. I'll try."

"Good for you," said Naomi. "Remember, like show jumping, the secret is keeping a good rhythm."

Naomi stood by the first small log, giving encouragement to Tilly and Rosie:

"That's it, Tilly. Stand up in your stirrups and get Rosie going forward and reacting to your leg."

Tilly approached the first fence nervously, concentrating hard.

When she was five strides away, she heard Naomi reminding her to sit in the saddle and keep her shoulders back.

"Very good, Tilly. Try not to grip with your knee – that will make your lower leg less secure."

Following Naomi's advice, over the second fence, Tilly's legs barely moved and Rosie flew over the brush fence. Then, sure enough, when Rosie got to the step, she knew exactly what to do. She hopped up neatly, had a quick look around, and then stepped off again. Tilly could hear the girls applauding from the side.

"That was fine," she said, surprised. "What's next?"

"Just have a rest for now – it's time for the others to have a go," said Naomi.

One by one, they each negotiated the various fences. Some were harder than others, but nothing seemed to faze Tilly and Rosie.

In fact, all was fine and smiles until they came to the final obstacle – the water ditch. Tilly overrode Rosie on the approach to the water ditch, which didn't give her pony enough time to see what she had to jump. Seeing the ditch at the last minute, Rosie spooked suddenly and stopped. Tilly lost her balance and immediately slid out of the saddle, ending up in the muddy water!

The girls gasped, but when they saw that Tilly was laughing, they realised she wasn't hurt. Rosie was standing patiently to the side, wondering what had happened to her rider.

"Oh well, one girl down, five more to go," said Naomi, grinning at the others. "Don't worry, Tilly. Water and ditches can often be tricky. With a bit more practice you'll be fine."

With that, Tilly re-mounted and approached the ditch again, more slowly this time, and with more leg pressure. She remembered to sit a little behind Rosie's movement, in what Naomi had called 'the safety seat position', and this time, Tilly was pleased when Rosie rewarded her by jumping over the ditch quite happily.

As the rest of the afternoon lesson progressed, Tilly wasn't the only one to fall off. The girls got more confident on the course, but they all took a tumble – even Sabrina, who also ended up in the muddy ditch, and was very cross about her new jodhpurs getting dirty.

"I've got an idea," said Mia. "Each fall should equal a bucket of cold water over the head! I heard the older guys talking about a water fight later."

"No one's throwing cold water over *me*," protested Sabrina.

"Better make sure you don't fall off again then," Mia said, giggling.

Tired but happy, the girls returned to the stables.

"Oh no!" Jessica moaned. "Tack cleaning!"

All Tilly wanted to do was crash on the sofa and play *Pony Ranch*. The thought of having to clean all her tack wasn't very appealing, especially since she was damp and muddy, but when she saw everyone sitting around, scrubbing and brushing, and talking about the day's adventures, she got into the spirit of it.

"My bum is *so* bruised," said Cally, as they walked back to the house.

"Mine too," came a chorus of voices after her.

"Buckets all round then," said Mia, winking.

Tea and homemade flapjacks revived everyone, and soon a whisper went around the dining hall that the water fight was about to start in the gardens. It was still sunny, so the girls rushed out, wearing t-shirts and shorts, and armed with plastic cups.

As soon as Tilly stepped through the door, a spray of freezing water drenched her. She shrieked and laughed.

"We need sponges!" yelled a voice.

"LOOK OUT!" came another, as a bucket of water poured down on Mia and Cally.

"Hey! We'll get you back for that," they threatened, but

when they saw the bucket
of water had come from
Brook, they both started
giggling and blushing.

In no time at all everyone was soaked.
The only person who didn't join in was
Sabrina. She watched from the window.

"Come on, Sabby," encouraged Brook,
tapping on the glass. "Don't think you're
going to spend the whole time hiding inside!"

Sabrina shook her head and mouthed
something about her hair extensions,
but before she could protest,
several of the older riders sneaked
in, picked her up and carried her
outside.

"Put me down! Put me
down!" she shrieked, but Tilly
could tell by the laughter in her
voice that she didn't mind *that*
much.

"Do you really want us to put
you down?" said one of the riders.

"Yes!" she squealed.

"*Really?*" he said again.

"*YES!*"

"Okay – you asked for it!"

With that, they carried her across the grass, over to the swimming pool, and surrounded by cheering, dropped her straight in.

SPLASH!

Sabrina bobbed to the surface, yelling at the top of her voice. Seconds later she was joined by most of the camp, who all dived or jumped into the pool fully-clothed.

"This is so much fun," gurgled Tilly, between mouthfuls of water.

Already Pony Club camp was proving to be the best holiday ever.

The only people who weren't so amused by the water fight were the camp organisers, Bob and Margaret. They sent everyone back to the house, to get dry and changed for supper.

"Honestly," grumbled Bob. "This happens every year. Will they *ever* learn?"

Eight

Every morning for the rest of the week, the alarm clocks buzzed at 7am. The girls crept out to the stables in their pyjamas, fed their ponies and mucked out their stalls. By the time they were changed and ready for breakfast, they were refreshed and alert, and they always looked forward to the tasty fry-ups. Even Tilly broke the habit of a lifetime, and ate sausages and bacon instead of muesli.

On Wednesday morning, Naomi told

Tilly and her group that they would be working on the Pony Club Dressage Test.

"Do we *have* to?" groaned Mia.

"Well, I can't wait. *I* love it," said Sabrina smugly. "My pony will do anything for me, and I'm part of a talent-spotting scheme."

Tilly wasn't sure what to think. She'd done a little bit of basic dressage with Angela before but didn't feel very confident about it, and of course she'd watched it on television endlessly.

"The word 'dressage'," explained Naomi, as the group gathered with their ponies at the indoor arena, "is French. It literally means 'training'. Riders perform a series of movements designed to show off a horse's natural athletic ability. Basically, it's about showing the judges that you can get your pony to do what you want him to, when you

want him to. Now, can anyone tell me what the letters around the arena mean?"

Tilly glanced at the painted letters on the arena walls. Feeling pleased, and a little relieved, to find she knew the answer, she raised her hand. Naomi nodded at her.

"They mark where different movements are to be performed."

"That's right. We're going to have some practice, and then you'll each get to ride the test."

The thought of this sparked a ripple of excitement from the girls, then they got straight to it, mounting their ponies and preparing for the first instruction. They practised serpentines from one end of the arena to the other, and then made transitions between the paces, adding in walks, canters, and turns.

Sabrina, Jessica, and Eleanor were the most experienced, so they worked down one end of the arena, while Naomi spent some time with Tilly, Mia and Cally, showing them how to make smooth transitions and then halt and salute.

"All the instruction should come from leg and seat signals," Naomi explained. "But they need to be subtle – the spectators shouldn't be able to see the signals being made."

Tilly urged Rosie forward with her leg, but all she did was shuffle. It was clear she wasn't in the mood for fancy footwork.

"It's as if she's stuck in treacle!" moaned Tilly. "She won't do anything for me today."

After struggling for twenty minutes, Tilly felt defeated.

"It's no good," she said. "I'm obviously useless at dressage."

"Hmm . . . I've got an idea," said Naomi. "I think it's time for a bit of a swap around."

Naomi arranged for all the girls to swap ponies for a while. This meant that Sabrina had to ride Rosie and Tilly got to ride Mr Fudge, while Cally rode Sabrina's pony, Angel. Mr Fudge's solid body felt strange to Tilly at first, because he was bigger and more athletic than Rosie, but Tilly soon found her balance.

Mr Fudge was very cooperative, and this time, Tilly got the responses she asked for. As she practised trotting and halting, she imagined what it must feel like to ride a top horse; then she thought of Magic Spirit, and suddenly missed him terribly. What was he doing?

she wondered. Was he still missing her?

"Keep concentrating, Tilly. You're doing really well, but don't lose focus. If you do that in front of the judges, your horse will be all over the place, and you'll lose marks!"

After a quick break for some orange squash and biscuits, the girls took turns to complete the tests that Naomi had planned for them. They got to ride their own ponies again, and as Tilly waited for her turn, she dreaded what kind of mess Rosie would make of it.

"Remember, I'll be giving you a mark out of ten for each movement," said Naomi, holding a clipboard to her chest. "I'll be awarding points for paces, rhythm, smoothness and precision, position and seat of rider, and correct use of the aids."

Tilly watched Sabrina and her pony, Angel, complete their test. She was amazed by how effortless they made everything look. Although Sabrina could be annoying and arrogant, she was clearly very talented.

She finished with an impressive square halt and everyone clapped.

Mia and Cally also did really well, and Mia got an eight out of ten for her free walk on a long rein, which she was thrilled about.

"Actually, I've always quite liked dressage," she said, smiling, after getting her results.

The first part of Tilly's test was an instruction to enter the arena in a working trot, and then proceed down the centre line

without halting. She then had to track left, transition into a walk for two to five steps, and return to a working trot. To her surprise, Rosie was much more obedient than before. She encouraged her along.

"That's it, girl, keep going!"

She then had to change the rein on the diagonal, which caused a bit of confusion, but she still managed to organise herself in time for the canter. She finished with a halt and salute, and, of course, a proud smile on her face.

"Congratulations, Tilly! For a first test, that was pretty good. And you were very balanced and straight in the halt. Well done!"

As they walked back to the main house for lunch, Tilly caught up with Sabrina.

"Thanks for sorting Rosie out for me," she said. "I don't know what you did with her, but it certainly made her perform better."

"Oh, it's no big deal," Sabrina replied.

"I'm used to riding different ponies. It's part of the Cavendish Hall programme. They think that if we get used to different rides, we'll develop better horsemanship. In modern pentathlon competitions, the riders don't know what horse they'll be using until an hour before they compete!"

"Blimey! That's hard."

"You get used to it."

"Do you want to be a top dressage competitor?"

"I want to be on the 2012 Olympic Dressage team. What about you?"

"I think I might like to be a three-day eventer, and take my favourite horse, Magic Spirit, to the Olympics one day. But ultimately, I'd love to run my own stables," said Tilly, wondering whether such a thing could ever come true for her.

Nine

Thursday was a fun day. The morning and afternoon riding sessions were gymkhana and mounted games. Everyone took part and enjoyed it.

"This may seem like a laugh," explained the camp organisers, Bob and Margaret, before the games began, "but these challenges are an excellent form of training for the ambitious young rider. You will need good hand-eye coordination, fierce determination and effective teamwork."

Tilly was pleased to take part in a real gymkhana. She had played the *Saddle Club Gymkhana* game on her PC hundreds of times. Her favourite event was tent-pegging, and her practice on the computer must have paid off, because when it came to her turn, she managed to pick up every hoop with her lance. Rosie enjoyed it too, and Tilly soon realised she was a much better gymkhana pony than a dressage pony!

As she was leaning on the fence, watching the others compete, Brook approached her. He was leading Solo.

"Hey, Tilly. I saw you competing. Well done for getting all the hoops. Do you know, I was looking at you and, well, you really remind me of someone. I can't think who it is though . . . Oh well, have you enjoyed your first camp so far?"

"It's been ace!" said Tilly. "I wish it could last for another week."

"Well, it's not quite finished yet. Tomorrow is competition day. We all have

to plait our horses, and then take part in a mini event: dressage, show jumping and cross-country."

"I like cross-country best," said Tilly.

"Me too," said Brook.

It was hard to fall asleep that night, with thoughts of the mini event turning over in Tilly's mind. Although she was exhausted from all the early starts and busy days, she kept worrying about whether she'd make it through the water or not.

Finally, her eyes shut and she was lost in a dream. When she woke next morning, she remembered her dream clearly: her real mum was standing with Brook and Solo, at the side of the cross-country track, watching her jump Magic Spirit over the dreaded ditch. It was strange but good.

No time to think about it though, because the girls had set their alarms extra early, so that they could be first in the yard, plaiting their ponies before breakfast.

"My plaits are lumpy!" said Mia, bleary-eyed. She couldn't get Sweetie's mane to look as neat as some of the other ponies.

"They need to be more evenly spaced," said Tilly. "Here, I'll show you."

Tilly managed to twist several perfect plaits.

"Takes practice, I guess," she shrugged, glancing at her own long dark plaits.

After breakfast, the girls dressed in their smartest riding gear, and went down to the stables, ready for the final inspection. Everyone stood next to their ponies, and waited for Bob and Margaret's comments.

"What neat braiding!" Margaret remarked, when she came to Sweetie. "Top marks for Mia and her pony."

Tilly and Mia winked at each other.

Tilly herself got praise for her neat
turn-out and clean tack, although Rosie
was marked down for her shaggy tail.

"I tried," Tilly said, sighing. "She's just
not a very elegant pony – but she's great at
gymkhanas!" She smiled and patted Rosie
on the shoulder.

Tilly stared down the line at the other
ponies. Some of them had very fancy
ribbons in their manes, and their owners
had all the best gear: fitted riding blazers,

shirts and ties, gloves, hair nets and boots that looked almost new.

Brook was standing at the end, with the senior riders. He looked very serious, as if he was about to take part in a major competition.

"Thank you, everybody," said Margaret, when they had finished judging. "We will be announcing the winners this evening, at the prize-giving ceremony. Good luck with the event. We've had a very high standard of riding this year, so I'm sure it will be a good one."

With that, everyone got into their groups and began leading their ponies out of the stables.

"Who do you think is going to win, then?" asked Mia, as they made their way to the training area.

"I reckon Sabrina will win the juniors' and Brook will win the seniors'," said Jessica.

Everyone agreed.

Sabrina beamed.

"Thanks, guys," she said. "I didn't think any of you liked me very much."

"We like you, Sabrina," said Mia. "You're just a bit . . . *fussy* sometimes, that's all."

"You're our number one hope," said Cally. "We'll all keep our fingers crossed for you."

"Hey," whispered Tilly, nudging Sabrina, "could you give me some tips for getting through that water?"

"Let Rosie work it out for herself. Don't force her forward. You'll be fine."

The junior groups competed first. Sabrina did a perfect dressage, as everyone knew she would. Her cross-country was also good, but she knocked a fence down in the jumping section.

"It's going to be close," whispered Eleanor, as they watched from the side.

"One of the girls in the other groups hasn't made a single fault so far."

"No one beats Sabrina in dressage."

Sabrina rode up, wearing a frown. She was obviously cross with herself.

"I can't believe I knocked that jump down! I've blown it now!"

"You haven't blown it," said Tilly. "You were great."

Moments later, Tilly heard her own name being called for the cross-country. Her stomach churned. She collected Rosie and made her way to the track. Although she knew she wasn't going to win the competition, it was still a chance to prove something. It was an opportunity to do her best and show everyone how much progress she had made. And if she always tried to do her best, maybe one day she *would* stand a chance of winning.

"Good luck, Tilly!" called a voice from across the track. Tilly turned and saw Brook waving at her from the fence. It was just like in her dream – except her mum

wasn't there.
Tilly thought of
the photograph
and tugged her
horsehair
bracelets.
Suddenly, it felt
as if her mum
was there in
spirit. She
stopped feeling
nervous and
knew what she
had to do.

Calmly, she
mounted Rosie,
whispered
encouragement,
and then approached the start box. As she
set off, she felt more confident than ever.
She got Rosie into a good canter, and
confidently jumped from fence to fence.
Until the only thing left was the water
jump.

Let Rosie work it out for herself. Don't force her forward. As the water came into view, Tilly could hear Sabrina's words in her head. She tried to relax, but somehow the effort of trying made her tense. Now the water was only a few strides away – just a matter of lining up and going for it. But the pressure was too much. As if sensing Tilly's worry, Rosie dodged the ditch and darted the other way.

Tilly's heart sank with disappointment.

"Give it another go!" called Brook.

"Go for it!" came a chorus of voices.

Tilly and Rosie circled then lined themselves up again. This time, Tilly tried not to think about 'trying' to relax. Instead, she fixed her mind on the image of her mums, both of them, and how proud they would be if they could see her now. She realised she was looking forward to seeing her family again and telling them all about her week; seeing Magic Spirit, and Lucky Chance, and Angela and Duncan.

And before she knew it, Tilly found herself striding into the water, up on to the opposite bank and then to the finish. Everyone cheered, especially Sabrina. It felt wonderful.

The day ended with a barbecue, followed by strawberry pavlova, which everyone agreed was the most delicious thing ever. Then it was time for the prize-giving. Bob and

Margaret had lots of awards
to give out. Mia won Best-
Groomed Junior Pony.
Eleanor came second. Cally
won an award for Best Team
Player during the mounted
events, and Jessica came second in the Junior
Show Jumping.

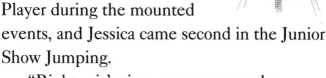

"Right – it's time to announce the
overall winners of the juniors and seniors,"
said Bob.

Tilly and the girls gathered round
Sabrina, linked arms, and then stood
perfectly still as they waited for the result.

"The overall winner of the juniors, with
one hundred and fifty-eight points, is . . ."

Mia clasped her hand to her mouth.

"Sabrina Belfonte!"

The girls jumped up and down
shrieking.

"I knew it," said Eleanor.

Sabrina collected her trophy and had to
stand at the front, while they announced
the senior champion.

"And the winner is . . . Brook Ashton-Smith!"

Everyone cheered again. The senior group members ruffled Brook's hair as he stepped through the crowd.

"He definitely deserves it," said Jessica. "He's so talented."

"And now," said Bob, "we have a special award for the young rider we think has shown the most improvement. All week we've been watching you, in both the junior and senior camps. This award goes to the individual who has really stood out – for their commitment, determination, and positive attitude."

"Who do you think it is?" whispered Mia.

"Don't know," shrugged Tilly. "I thought they'd given out all the awards."

"This is an individual," added Margaret, "who has shown great potential, and that's something we always look out for at Pony Club. The winner of our Most Improved award is . . . Tilly Redbrow!"

Tilly gasped.

For a moment she couldn't move then she felt her friends' hands surrounding her, pushing her forward. She stumbled to the front and accepted the shiny silver cup that Bob and Margaret presented.

"Well done!" they said, shaking her hand.

Brook and Sabrina congratulated her, and then the three of them had their photograph taken. Tilly felt like a real champion, with cameras flashing and everyone applauding her. It was the perfect ending to a perfect camp.

Ten

The following morning everyone struggled out of bed, but there was no time to waste because everything had to be packed and ready to leave by midday.

"I'm more tired today than any other day," moaned Mia, yawning. Her hair was all over the place.

"That's because we're leaving and none of us wants to go," said Jessica. "Once we get out of bed and go down to the stables, it's the start of the end!"

"Well, I think you're tired because you've been up all night giggling and eating strawberry laces," grumbled Sabrina. "Personally, I'm ready to go home – I'm looking forward to a proper pillow and no one to keep me awake all night!"

"Let's just get it over with, shall we?" said Tilly. "At least we've got one more yummy breakfast to enjoy!"

Tilly was sad that camp was coming to an end. She'd loved every minute of it and learned so much, but her thoughts quickly turned to Silver Shoe Farm. Magic would be waiting for her and she looked forward to telling him every little detail about camp. And of course, she'd get to see Lucky Chance again. Had she grown? Tilly wondered. Was she trotting more? Galloping to and fro?

Suddenly the idea of seeing Lucky playing in the long field, and talking to Magic made Tilly feel a whole lot better about going home.

Tilly shuffled out to the stables. The sky was grey and it was starting to rain – it really did feel like the end of camp. She fed Rosie and cleaned the stables one last time. She also made sure she gave Rosie several peppermints. Rosie deserved a treat, now that she had helped Tilly win her first Pony Club award.

"You were brilliant yesterday," she said, stroking Rosie's mane. "You may not be the sportiest pony in the world, but you're definitely one of the nicest!"

Tilly kissed Rosie goodbye, packed up her kit, and then met the others over in the dining hall.

"I can't believe it's over," said Jessica, spreading marmite on her toast. "I'm gutted!"

"I'm going to miss everyone so much," said Cally.

"We'll have to get together at the next Pony Club event," said Eleanor. "We should go and watch Sabrina in her dressage competitions."

"Good idea."

This suggestion cheered everyone up. They made a pact to stay in contact, and maybe even meet up for a few hacks. The Cavendish Hall girls said there were some great rides near their school. Then it was time to pack the suitcases, and load up the horses.

By eleven-thirty, everything was ready. The campers gathered outside and said goodbye to their instructors.

"Thanks for everything, Naomi," said Tilly. "You've given me some really good ideas."

"No problem. Keep riding, Tilly. And well done for getting your prize – you deserve it. Will we see you next year?"

"Definitely!"

"Okay. Everyone climb on board!" called the driver. "It's time!"

Slowly, Tilly turned and stepped on to the bus. Her legs were so heavy with tiredness that it was hard to lift them. Maybe Sabrina was right, she thought. She'd loved every minute of Pony Club camp, but right now, a comfortable bed and a long lie in seemed very appealing.

As the girls arranged themselves on the bus, taking over the two back rows, they agreed that they would make the most of the hour-long journey by singing all the way. They made a list of songs including

hits by all their favourite artists. They even offered to do special requests, and went round asking the others what they'd like to hear, but by the time the engine started and the bus was purring away from Barton House, the two back rows were silent. They were all fast asleep, lost in their dreams. And Tilly, of course, was dreaming of Magic Spirit.

Pippa's Top Tips

Foaling usually happens any time between 10pm and 4am. There's no need to interfere, but always have a vet on call just in case the mare gets into any difficulties.

It's normal for there to be some bleeding after the breaking of the umbilical cord. Iodine solution applied to the foal's belly will prevent infection.

The mare will generally drop her placenta within three hours of foaling. Make sure you keep this so the vet can examine it and check everything is normal.

Exercise helps enormously with a foal's development, so try to ensure he spends plenty of time at pasture. This will also allow the foal to build his confidence around the other horses.

Pony Club camp is an ideal learning environment. Watch the other riders, pick up new techniques and learn from each other's mistakes.

When practising cross-country, remember not to get too far forward with your balance, because if your pony stops, hits a fence, or stumbles on landing, you'll more than likely end up on the ground!

Jumping water and ditches can often be tricky. Approach slowly, apply leg pressure, and sit a little behind your pony's movement in the safety seat position. Don't force your pony forward, let him work the jump out for himself.

The word 'dressage' is French for 'training'. Riders perform a series of movements designed to show off a horse's natural athletic ability. Points are awarded for pace, rhythm, smoothness and precision, position and seat of rider, and correct use of the aids.

If you can, try to ride different ponies. Getting used to different rides will help you develop better horsemanship.

Gymkhanas are great fun, and also an excellent form of training for young riders. You'll need good hand-eye coordination, fierce determination and effective teamwork in order to succeed.

For more about Tilly and Silver Shoe Farm –
including pony tips, quizzes and everything
you ever wanted to know about horses –
visit www.tillysponytails.co.uk